First published in Japanese as *Aru hareta hi ni* by Kodansha Ltd. in 1996.

Distributed in the United States by Kodansha America, Inc., 575 Lexington Avenue, New York, N.Y. 10022, and in the United Kingdom and continental Europe by Kodansha Europe Ltd., 95 Aldwych, London WC2B 4JF. Published by Kodansha International Ltd., 17-14, Otowa 1-chome, Bunkyo-ku, Tokyo 112-8652, and by Kodansha America, Inc.

First edition, 2003
ISBN 4-7700-2971-3
03 04 05 06 07 10 9 8 7 6 5 4 3 2 1

www.thejapanpage.com

ONE SUNNY DAY...

STORY BY **YUICHI KIMURA**

PICTURES BY **HIROSHI ABE**

TRANSLATION BY LUCY NORTH

KODANSHA INTERNATIONAL
Tokyo • New York • London

Not a cloud was in sight, just clear blue skies for as far as the eye could see. Little birds flew to and fro excitedly, and all the flowers and leaves on the trees shone with drops of rain.

On this utterly peaceful afternoon, which made last night's blustery storm seem like a dream, the figures of two animals could be seen climbing a hill.

And they were laughing merrily.

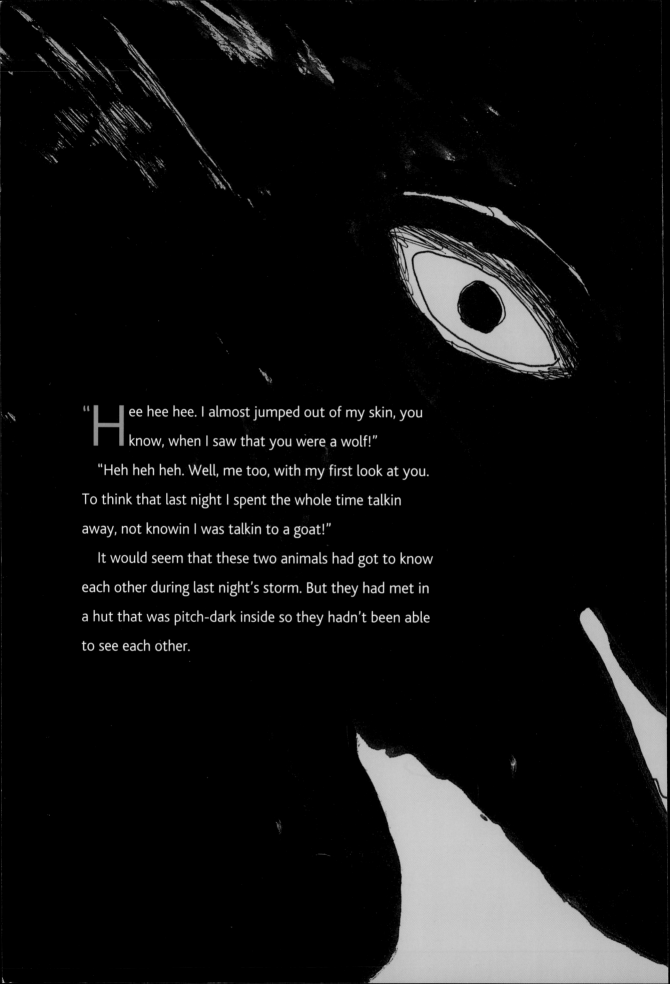

"Hee hee hee. I almost jumped out of my skin, you know, when I saw that you were a wolf!"

"Heh heh heh. Well, me too, with my first look at you. To think that last night I spent the whole time talkin away, not knowin I was talkin to a goat!"

It would seem that these two animals had got to know each other during last night's storm. But they had met in a hut that was pitch-dark inside so they hadn't been able to see each other.

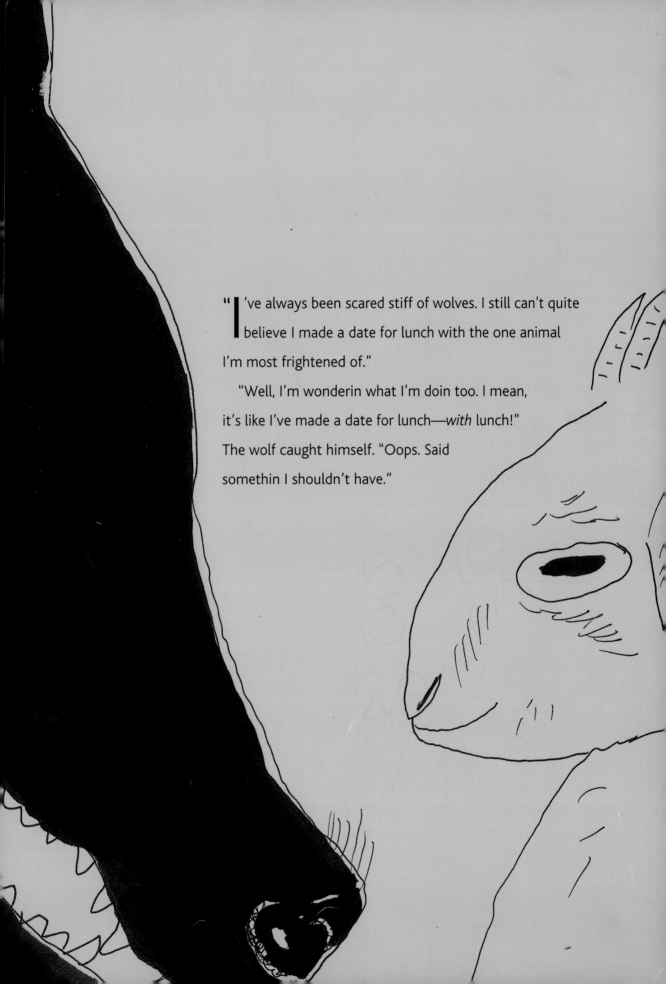

"I've always been scared stiff of wolves. I still can't quite believe I made a date for lunch with the one animal I'm most frightened of."

"Well, I'm wonderin what I'm doin too. I mean, it's like I've made a date for lunch—*with* lunch!" The wolf caught himself. "Oops. Said somethin I shouldn't have."

"That's all right. I know if you really wanted to gobble me up, you'd have done so just now, when we met in front of the hut."

"True. I might look like yer typical wolf, but for me, friendship comes first, before anythin else."

"Really? Me too. See? We've got so much in common. And we were both so frightened by the thunder last night."

The two of them were climbing the hill at quite a pace.

At the very top there was an outcrop of rocks, and here they were going to eat the packed lunch that they had each brought with them.

All of a sudden the goat started to giggle.

"What? What's so funny?"

"I was remembering just now when I was waiting in the bushes round the tree in front of the hut."

"Yes, that was the meetin place we agreed on."

"You came up to the tree from the other side, and said, 'Stormy Night.'"

"Yeah, 'Stormy Night' was the password we chose, as we didn't know what we looked like, it was so dark."

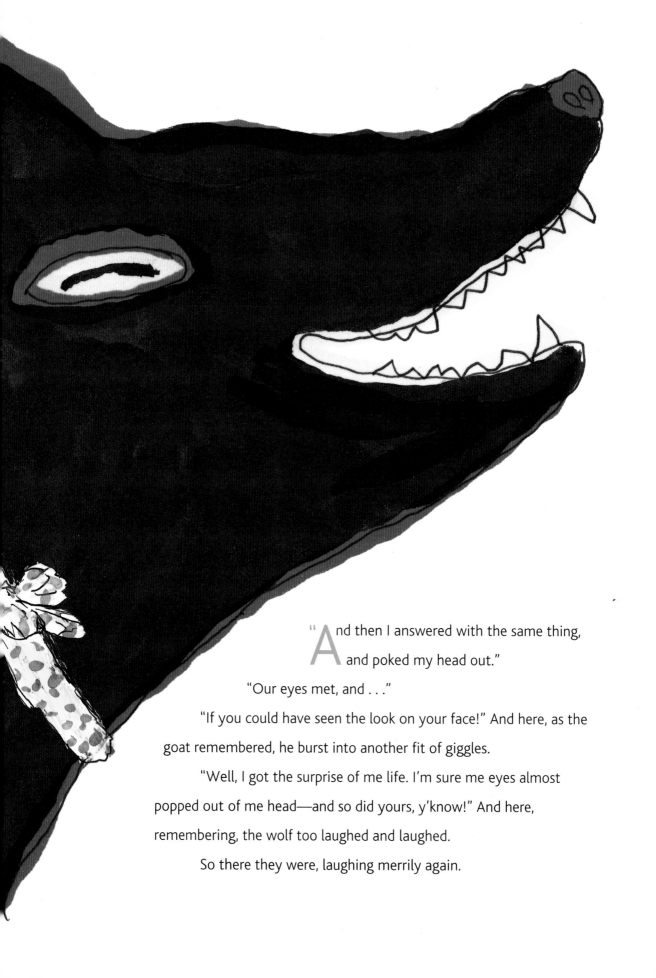

"And then I answered with the same thing, and poked my head out."

"Our eyes met, and . . ."

"If you could have seen the look on your face!" And here, as the goat remembered, he burst into another fit of giggles.

"Well, I got the surprise of me life. I'm sure me eyes almost popped out of me head—and so did yours, y'know!" And here, remembering, the wolf too laughed and laughed.

So there they were, laughing merrily again.

"Now here you should watch your step," the goat warned. "If you lose your footing, you'll tumble right to the bottom of the ravine."

"Heh heh," the wolf replied cheerily. "The other fellers

The goat sighed. "I did tell you to be careful."

"Heh heh," the wolf laughed. "Bit stupid of me. But it doesn't matter. We wolves, see, we can go for two or three days on an empty stomach. We're pretty tough."

He forced himself to laugh again. But the truth was, this wolf had an appetite. A *large* appetite.

On and on they climbed. The sun was no longer directly overhead, but inclined a little toward the west. The mountain path got narrower and narrower.

"From here on, we've got to go single file, so I'll go first," the goat told the wolf.

"Right. On you go, then," the wolf answered, forcing himself to be cheerful. In actual fact, though, he was starting to feel quite ravenous.

Ah well, he was thinking. No lunch for me. Just have to grin and bear it.

At that moment, he looked up, and there, right in front of his eyes, was the goat's bottom.

And every time the goat jumped up to another rock along the path, his bottom waggled and bobbed.

And his tail, which looked as if it would make quite a tender, tasty morsel, swung to and fro, just as if it were enticing the wolf to try and take a snap at it.

"Mm. I'd love to have a bite of *that*. . ." The wolf couldn't stop his mouth watering at the sight. He gulped back his saliva.

The next moment, though, he shook his head.

"Oh dear! What a bad character I've got!" he muttered to himself. "To even think for a second that a friend was a tasty-lookin snack!"

And he gave himself several raps on the head with his paws for even thinking such a bad thought.

After that, he took care to keep his eyes fixed on the ground as he climbed up the path.

"We're nearly there. See the top?" The goat looked back over his shoulder with a smile. The wolf forced himself to look up and smile back.

"Wow, what a view! Look, we can see all the way to Fleecy Valley."

"Yeah, look at that. That's where I go with the other fellers from the pack and . . ." Get ourselves tasty snacks, was what the wolf was about to say, but he stopped himself, and his mouth snapped shut.

By tasty snacks, of course, he meant goats.

"Well, let's not waste any time—let's have our picnic!" said the goat. "Oh, sorry. I forgot. You dropped yours."

"That's right," the wolf said, trying as hard as he could to look somewhere else—anywhere but the goat in front of him.

"You're always welcome to share some of my grass. Here, have half of it. But I suppose you really want meat, don't you? Come to think of it, the packed lunch you dropped may have been meat. . . Not, by any chance . . . goat meat?"

"'Course not! If there's one kind of meat I can't stand, it's goat. I'd have thought that'd be obvious."

In fact, the wolf was very fond of goat meat. It was one of his favorite foods.

"Eat," he said. "Don't mind me. I'll just take a little nap."

And he flung himself down as if he couldn't care less. In fact, though, he was so hungry that the last thing on his mind was sleep.

"Will you just look at that view! You couldn't ask for anything more, could you—the best view in the world as you eat your lunch," remarked the goat. "It's fantastic. Hey! Gone to sleep already? That was pretty quick."

The wolf was in fact listening to the goat chattering behind him, as he lay there on the ground.

Hmph! he said to himself. My picnic actually came with me all the way, and there it is right behind me still. The only reason I can't eat it is 'cos—well, my lunch is my friend.

And he laughed to himself at his private joke, and kept his eyes shut tight.

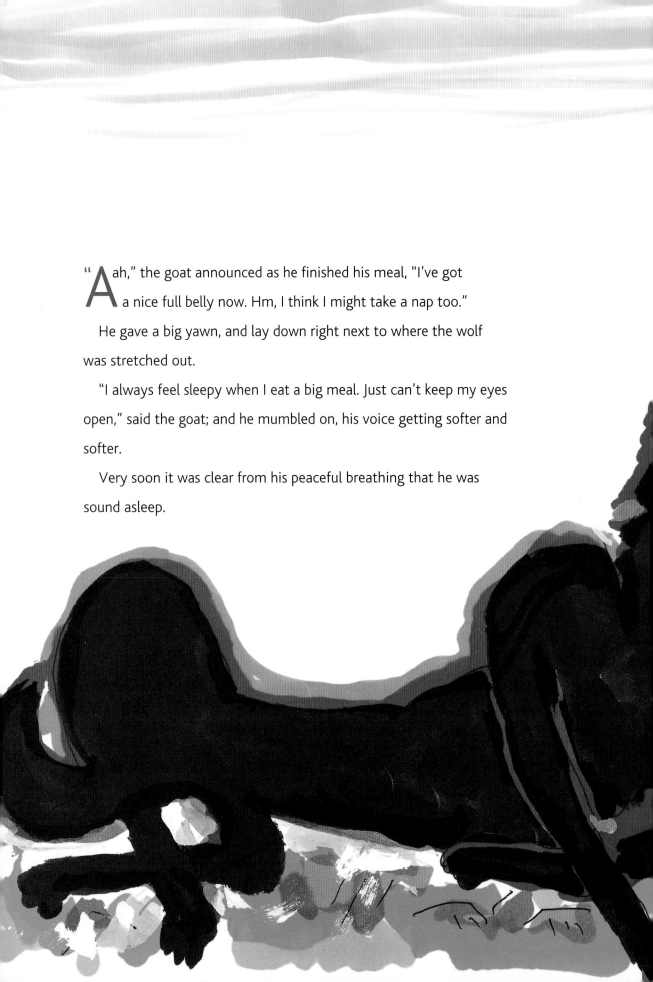

"Aah," the goat announced as he finished his meal, "I've got a nice full belly now. Hm, I think I might take a nap too."

He gave a big yawn, and lay down right next to where the wolf was stretched out.

"I always feel sleepy when I eat a big meal. Just can't keep my eyes open," said the goat; and he mumbled on, his voice getting softer and softer.

Very soon it was clear from his peaceful breathing that he was sound asleep.

At which point the wolf sat up abruptly,
and stared down at the sleeping goat.
He stared at him for a long time.

"It'd be much easier if I didn't like him so much. He *would* make a tasty mouthful, but somehow I just enjoy being with him. I do love the taste of goat, though. . . Ooh, one of his ears twitched. Now if I could just take a li-t-t-le bite of that . . . He might even allow me a chew, offer me a bit as a friend. Well, maybe not, but . . . But I am hungry, and . . ."

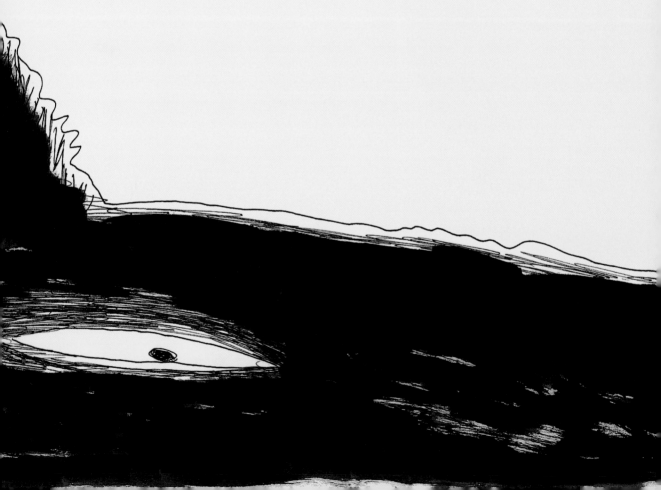

And stealthily the wolf stretched over and brought his muzzle close to the goat's ear.

"Just a little nibble wouldn't hurt. But then, I can't help thinkin it would. He'd bleed. And he wouldn't feel the same way about me any more—his feelins would definitely change. . ." And the wolf gave a wistful sigh.

"Ee hee hee!" the goat tittered sleepily. "Stop blowing in my ear, would you? It tickles!"

He opened his eyes, now wide awake.

"I'm a very ticklish person. You just have to touch me and it starts. My ears are especially ticklish. Ah, that nap's made me feel much better. Well, maybe we ought to be on our way soon."

The goat gave himself a good stretch and stood up.

"What? Oh, yes. Yes," the wolf replied casually, but his eyes had a very strange expression, a definite glint. This came as quite a shock to the goat.

So he *was* thinking about eating me, he thought.

The next moment, though, he shook his head.

"Oh dear! What a bad character I've got!" he muttered to himself. "To even think for a second that my friend could do that!"

And he gave himself several raps on the head with his hooves for even thinking such a bad thought.

Soon after the two animals started their descent, the sky suddenly grew dark.

"Looks like there's gonna be a rainstorm," the wolf remarked.

"Oh, it'll only be a shower, I'm sure."

"Don't know about that. Thought I saw a flash of somethin just now."

"Oh no! Not . . . ?!"

There was a loud roll of
thunder.
"Yikes!"
"He-e-e-lp!"
Both animals yelled out in fright,
and made a mad dash together down the
hillside.
Great big drops of rain started to
splash down one after the other.
The two of them found a small cave,
in which they quickly took shelter.

"I hate thunder more than anything else in the world!"

"Me too!"

There was another long roll of thunder.

"Oh!" gasped the goat.

"Ah!" gasped the wolf.

The thunder rumbled on and on, and the two clutched each other, waiting for it to pass.

RUM-M-M-BLE!!

As they sat there holding each other tight, the smell of the goat began to fill the wolf's nostrils and spread to every corner of his head.

His belly started to growl.

ROAR went the thunder.

"Oh!" both animals gasped.

And they held on tighter to each other.

Then the wolf's belly g-r-o-w-l-ed.

Roar!

"Oh!"

Squeeze.

G-r-o-w-l.

This roaring, gasping, squeezing, and growling continued for—well, for goodness knows how long.

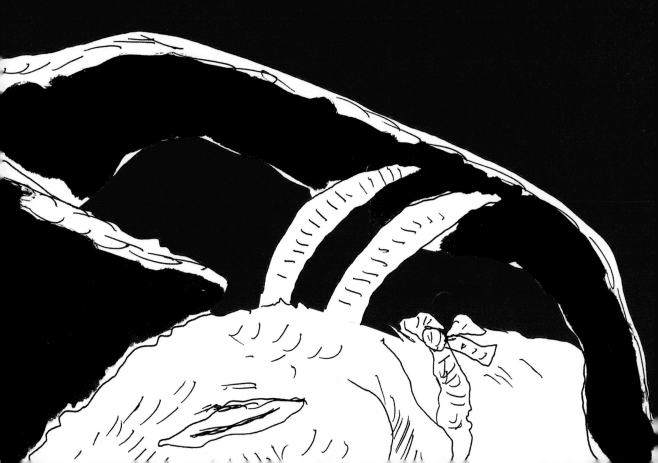

Finally, the big rain clouds went on their way,
and some rays of sunshine poked through.
Everything went perfectly quiet inside the cave.
And then, suddenly, there was a scream!

A high, shrill bleating from deep inside it, which
could be heard quite far away.
And then some little moans of pain. . .

After a short while, there was the scritch-scratch of the wolf's paws on the rocky floor of the cave.

Finally, the wolf poked his head out of the entrance.

"Never heard anythin like it. Slippin and hurtin yerself like that!"

"I know. I do feel a bit silly. Sorry." And there the goat was, smiling, a little embarrassed, being carried along on the wolf's back.

The steep, rocky hillside made the going rough enough as it was, but the wolf had an empty belly, and now he had to carry the goat on his shoulders. One step at a time, he picked his way carefully down the path.

"You were lucky this time 'cos I was with you. You should watch yer step more."

"I always have been a bit careless. But you can put me down now. Thanks. Just a little further down the path, we'll have to take our different turnings."

The wolf was silent as he gently let the goat down off his shoulders.

By the time they neared the bottom of the hill, the evening sun was starting to sink below the horizon.

"Well. I go this way." The goat waved his hoof in farewell.

The wolf said nothing and simply watched as the goat went off.

His belly gave a rumble. A *loud* rumble.

The wolf turned to go up his own path, but then stopped and looked back.

His belly rumbled again, even more loudly.

"I just have to. Can't help it," he muttered. And the next moment he was off and running, heading straight toward the goat.

He overtook him in a second. He opened his jaws very wide, and—

After taking a big breath to steady himself,
he said:

"We forgot to talk about somethin
important."

"Really?" The goat looked up at him.
"Remind me what it was."

There was a pause.

"Er . . ."

The wolf looked down at the
ground and then forced himself
to say, in a shy, hesitant voice:
"So when're we gonna meet again?"

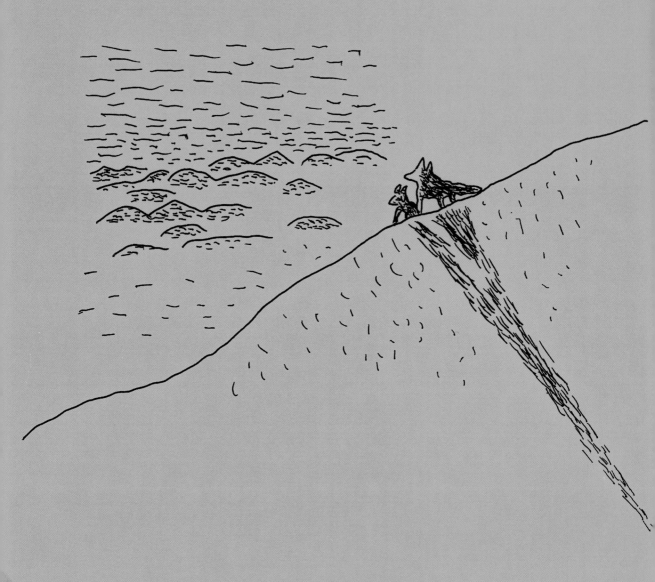

In the light of the evening sun, the shadows cast by the two animals on the grass joined to form one long shadow that stretched for a long way over the hillside.